Published by Scholastic Inc.
90 Old Sherman Turnpike, Danbury, Connecticut 06816.

For information regarding permission, write to:
Disney Licensed Publishing
114 Fifth Avenue, New York, New York 10011.

ISBN 0-7172-7764-X

Designed and produced by Bill SMITH STUDIO.

Printed in the U.S.A.
First printing, September 2002

Sweet Success

A Story About Sharing

by **Jacqueline A. Ball**
illustrated by
Caveman Productions

SCHOLASTIC INC.

New York   Toronto London Auckland Sydney
Mexico City   New Delhi   Hong Kong   Buenos Aires

"All finished," said Cinderella, holding up a drawing of a cake for her mice friends to see.

"Pretty, Cinderelly!" admired Jaq.

"Pretty-pretty," echoed Gus, who was busy piling up berries.

"I'm going to bake a cake like this for the festival tomorrow," Cinderella told them. "I've already measured and put aside all the ingredients."

*E*very year the village held a festival to celebrate the King's birthday. The most popular event was His Royal Highness's Most Supremely Special Birthday Cake contest. The judge was none other than the King himself!

"Mistress Muffin usually wins," Cinderella told Jaq. "But—"

"CINDERELLLLA!" a voice interrupted from downstairs. "*Where* is our lunch?"

"Coming, Stepmother," Cinderella called. She stuffed the drawing in her apron pocket and dashed down the stairs.

In the kitchen, Cinderella quickly made lunch. "Here, Jaq and Gus," she said, handing them a small piece of cheese. "Share this with your friends." She picked up a tray and hurried through the door to the dining room.

"*W*hat took you so long?" asked her Stepmother. Her eyes fell on the paper in Cinderella's apron pocket. She leaned forward and snatched it. "Hmm. What have we here?"

"*I*t's an idea I had for a cake," Cinderella
explained, "for the festival."

Cinderella's Stepmother gave her a mean
little smile. "You may have permission to make
a cake . . .

. . . *After* you completely clean the house from top to bottom and *after* my daughters have baked their own prize-winning creations," her Stepmother finished.

With a wink, she passed Cinderella's sketch to Anastasia and Drizella.

*C*inderella scrubbed and swept and polished and dusted. Finally, she finished. "I barely have time to bake my cake. It's a good thing I've already put aside all the ingredients."

Just then two voices screeched from the kitchen: "CINDERELLLLLLLLLA!"

"Oh, my!" Cinderella exclaimed as she entered the kitchen.

"*S*he made *me* ruin *my* cake!" shouted both sisters at once.

Two cakes were on the table. One was as flat as a pancake. One was burnt to a crisp.

"Let's clean up this mess, and you can start again," said Cinderella kindly. She began to sweep.

"*I*'m not cleaning!" said Anastasia.
She grabbed the measuring cups from her
sister—and slipped on some eggs. *CRASH!*

"*W*ell, I'm not cleaning either!" shouted Drizella.

She snatched a mixing bowl—and slipped on some spilled sugar. *SMASH!*

"Look what *you've* done!" both sisters shouted at each other.

Cinderella shook her head. The sacks were half empty. Many eggs were broken. There weren't enough ingredients left to make another big cake.

Cinderella paused. The ingredients she'd put aside were hidden away under a tablecloth. She could share them with her stepsisters. But then she would not have enough to make a big cake of her own.

*W*hat would a Princess do?

"*I* know," Cinderella said softly. "You can have some of *my* ingredients and make one large cake together."

Greedily the sisters pounced on them. They mixed and stirred and poured, threw everything into a pan, and soon they had a cake. Well, it was sort of a cake.

"*I*t's gorgeous!" bragged Anastasia.

"It's prize-winning," added Drizella.

"It's done!" whispered Jaq to Gus.

The stepsisters left, leaving Cinderella to clean up once again. She sighed as she saw how few ingredients were left!

*J*ust then Jaq and Gus got her attention.

"Here, Cinderelly. For you!" they called.

She looked down and saw little piles of berries, nuts, flowers, and other things.

"You share with us—" Gus began.

"And we share with you," finished Jaq.

"Oh, how sweet," said Cinderella. "Thank you!"

Cinderella stirred nuts and berries into a honey-sweetened mixture and baked it. Then she decorated her cake with flowers.

"It's not what I planned," she thought. "But it's special because my friends shared their food with me to help make it."

*T*he next morning the stepsisters rushed into the kitchen, arguing.

"*I'll* carry it, Anastasia!"

"No, *I'll* carry it!"

They tugged and yanked and pushed and pulled until . . .

*S*PLAT!

"Now we'll never win!" wailed Drizella.

"It's all your fault!" screamed Anastasia.

The sisters glared at each other above the

ruined cake.

"You can share my cake," Cinderella offered. "We can all enter it together!"

The stepsisters glanced down their noses at the small cake. "*That* puny pile of crumbs?" sniffed Anastasia.

Drizella folded her arms. "I'd rather not go at all."

So Cinderella went to the festival with only her animal friends for company.

Cinderella placed her cake on a long table. "Oh, dear," she thought. "My cake does look small compared to the others."

Just then trumpets sounded.
The judging was about to begin!
Slowly the King made his way
down the line of cakes. He took
a bite of each one.

When the King tasted Cinderella's cake, he smiled. He took a second bite. He whispered to the Duke.

Next he took a bite of the big, castle-shaped cake made by Mistress Muffin.

The King continued taking bites of the two cakes, first Cinderella's, then Mistress Muffin's.

Everyone at the festival wondered which cake the King would choose.

"*T*he winner of His Royal Highness's Most Supremely Special Birthday Cake contest is— Mistress Muffin!" announced the Duke.

"But Cinderelly," protested Jaq, "your cake was the best!"

"Now, now," said Cinderella. "The King has chosen well."

Then the trumpets sounded once again.

"*B*ut," called the Duke. "For a cake as natural and fresh as the forest, whose delectable, delicious distinction has delighted the royal taste buds—a special prize goes to Cinderella!"

Cinderella brought cake home for all her friends to share. That night, they all gathered round. And Cinderella, Jaq, and Gus shared the story of their sweet success.

The End